Many Colors of Me

Breathing in a Rainbow of Feelings

By Dawn Gallahue

Illustrated by Michaela Foster

AuthorHouse™
1663 Liberty Drive
Bloomington, IN 47403
www.authorhouse.com
Phone: 1 (800) 839-8640

Published by AuthorHouse 08/25/2016

ISBN: 978-1-5246-1339-6 (sc)
ISBN: 978-1-5246-1338-9 (e)

Library of Congress Control Number: 2016909405

Print information available on the last page.

Any people depicted in stock imagery provided by Thinkstock are models,
and such images are being used for illustrative purposes only.
Certain stock imagery © Thinkstock.

This book is printed on acid-free paper.

authorHOUSE®

This book is dedicated to my son, Noah and my angel nephew, baby Trent. May your generation bring love and healing to the earth and all humanity. May you pave the way for open, loving and forgiving hearts for all of mankind.

P.S. Uncle Paul, I really did it!

To:

This book belongs to:

All of the Children

Peace, love and rainbows!

Dawn Galleur ♡

The pouring rain has slowed to a sprinkle, and the sun is starting to shine. The raindrops glisten in the sun, and a beautiful rainbow appears in the sky.

Noah is looking out the window and feels sad and as gray as
the clouds outside. He could use a little cheering up, so he puts
on his boots, grabs his umbrella and runs out the door.

Noah starts to feel better as he splashes around in the puddles.
Off in the distance he sees the bright, colorful rainbow.

The rainbow is awesome! Noah notices a magical spot underneath, and runs over to explore it. He is curious, and wonders if the colors have magical powers.

As Noah stands under the rainbow, he feels the
amazing energy and magic it gives off. Now he knows
the colors have powerful, healing meanings, and he
prepares to receive them. He is so excited!

He closes his eyes and says, "I breathe in the color RED right through my nose, down through my body, and out through my toes."

*For each color, breathe in through YOUR nose after you say "nose," and exhale through YOUR mouth after you say "toes."

The red fills him up, and he feels full of
COURAGE. He is PEACEFUL and PATIENT.
Noah feels so connected to nature.

"I breathe in the color ORANGE right through my nose, down through my body, and out through my toes."

The orange fills him up, and he feels NICE. He is so
FRIENDLY and likes to COOPERATE with others.

"I breathe in the color YELLOW right through my nose,
down through my body, and out through my toes."

The yellow fills him up, and he feels WORTHY of greatness.
He is CONFIDENT and POWERFUL.

"I breathe in the color GREEN right through my nose,
down through my body, and out through my toes."

The green fills him up, and he feels so much LOVE!
His world is full of JOY and HAPPINESS.

"I breathe in the color BLUE right through my nose,
down through my body, and out through my toes."

The blue fills him up, and he feels POSITIVE.
He is HONEST and CARING.

"I breathe in the color **INDIGO** right through my nose,
down through my body, and out through my toes."

The indigo fills him up, and he feels **THOUGHTFUL**.
He is **WISE** and has a great **IMAGINATION**.

"I breathe in the color **PURPLE** right through my nose,
down through my body, and out through my toes."

The purple fills him up, and he feels CREATIVE and KIND.
His world is full of BEAUTY, both inside and out.

Wow, the colors of the rainbow are incredible! Noah went from feeling sad and gray to being filled with a rainbow of positive feelings! Noah LOVES himself UNCONDITIONALLY. He jumps up and shouts with a smile, "I feel COMPLETE!"

COURAGEOUS   NICE
PEACEFUL   FRIENDLY
PATIENT   COOPERATIVE

LOVE   WORTHY
JOYFUL   CONFIDENT
HAPPY   POWERFUL

                    THOUGHTFUL
                    WISE
POSITIVE   IMAGINATIVE
HONEST
CARING

CREATIVE
KIND
BEAUTIFUL   UNCONDITIONAL LOVE
                    COMPLETE

Special thanks to my amazing illustrator Michaela Foster, a talented young person who will be attending Montserrat School of Art in the fall of 2016. Michaela is a published artist as well as an aspiring cartoonist and animator.

I'd also like to thank my husband Adam, Rev. Terry Shaw, my sister Amber, and Lil' Mamas for your constant support, encouragement and feedback. Special thanks to my "secret advisory board" – mom, dad, EE, MB, CAR, MC, ML, JU, MK, AA, MF, EG and the Als.

Dawn Gallahue is an author from Marshfield, MA who writes from Naples, FL. Before pursuing her dreams, Dawn spent over 15 years in health care as a Registered EEG Tech and Registered Sleep Tech specializing in pediatrics. In addition to writing, she is also a life coach, a licensed massage therapist, and a loving mother with an innate passion for traveling, inspiring, and learning. When she isn't writing, Dawn likes being in the great outdoors and capturing precious moments with her camera.

To learn more about Dawn, visit www.dawngal.com.

Get your FREE MP3 Audio
version of the story by visiting:
www.dawngal.com/ManyColorsofMeAudio

CPSIA information can be obtained
at www.ICGtesting.com
Printed in the USA
BVOW05s1213230317

479238BV00004B/5/P